CENTRAL POINT

DATE DUE

DEC 7 '9	APR 17 '01		
JAN 1 2 '9	NOV 1 4 '00		
JAN 1 2 '95	JUN 06 '02		
AUG 1 6 '95	JUL 08 '02		
SEP 1 9 '95	NOV 2 2 '02		
	DEC 1 1 200		
OCT 1 7 '95			
AUG 0 4 '9			
OCT 2 7 '9			
NOV 3 '97			
JUL 12 '99			
NOV 4 '99			

The King at the Door

The KING at the DOOR

words and pictures by
Brock Cole

DOUBLEDAY & COMPANY, INC., GARDEN CITY, NEW YORK

Library of Congress Catalog Card Number 78-20064

ISBN: 0-385-14718-X Trade
ISBN: 0-385-14719-8 Prebound

"Master! Master!" cried Little Baggit. "The King is at the door!"

What a flurry there was!

The innkeeper, his wife, and the servant girl all rushed to the window, but all they saw was an old man in a patched shirt, sitting on the bench beside the door.

"That old beggar?" said the innkeeper. "If he's the King, where's his golden crown?"

"He left it at the palace because it's too heavy," said Little Baggit, "but he's the King, all right. He told me he was."

"Oh, he *told* you he was the King? Well, that's different," said the innkeeper. "He must be the King, then, mustn't he? And what does His Majesty desire?"

"He wants a glass of wine," said Little Baggit. "He's been walking over his roads all day counting the milestones, and he's thirsty."

"And how will he pay?" asked the innkeeper. "I suppose he left his bags of gold at the palace, too."

"That's right!" said Little Baggit. "How did you guess? He says he'll send the money tomorrow by royal coach."

"Oh yes, of course he will! We can trust the King, can't we? Here," said the innkeeper, "give him this."

"That?" cried Little Baggit. "But that's dishwater!"

"Yes, indeed!" said the innkeeper. "Very soothing for the parched throat. The soap makes it go down easier."

"Well," said Little Baggit, "you know better than I," and he took the glass of dishwater to the old man.

After a while he came back.

"Master," he said, "the King didn't like the dishwater."

"Oh mildew," said the innkeeper. "Whatever shall I do?"

"Don't worry," said Little Baggit. "I gave him the ale I was saving for my supper. He said that was fine."

"That was smart of you, Little Baggit. You're quicker than a moonbeam," said the innkeeper. "I suppose now the King would like a bite to eat."

"How did you guess? That's exactly what he would like."

"Then give him this," said the innkeeper.

"That?" said Little Baggit. "But that's the dog's dinner."

"Of course it is! I save all the best bits for old Towser because I love him better than anything."

"Well, you know better than I," said Little Baggit, and he took the dog's dinner to the old man.

After a while he came back.

"Master," he said, "the King didn't like the dog's dinner."

"Wilting lettuce! Whatever shall I do?" cried the innkeeper.

"Don't worry," said Little Baggit. "I gave him the loaf I was saving for my supper. He liked that fine."

"Little Baggit, you are sounder than a dinner bell," said the inn-keeper. "Does His Majesty desire anything else?"

"Why, yes, he does. How did you guess? He needs a hat to keep the sun from shining in his eyes."

"Of course!" said the innkeeper. "We can't have the sun shining on the King's bald head. Here. Take him this."

"That? But that's an old cooking pot."

"Yes indeed! The best kind of hat there is. It will wear like iron."

"Well," said Little Baggit, "you know better than I," and he took the iron pot to the old man.

After a while he came back.

"Master, the King didn't like the iron pot."

"Oh burnt potatoes," cried the inn-keeper. "Whatever shall I do?"

"Don't worry," said Little Baggit. "I gave him my hat, and he said that it would do fine."

"Thank goodness, Little Baggit," said the innkeeper. "You're sharper than a frog's tooth. I suppose His Majesty would like to borrow a coat, too."

"I never!" said Little Baggit. "How did you guess? That's just what he needs to keep the evening chill off on his way to the palace."

"I thought so," said the innkeeper. "Here. Give him this."

"That? But that's the old coat the dog sleeps on."

"Little Baggit, this was the coat I was married in. Could there be any garment that I value more?"

"Well," said Little Baggit, "you know better than I," and he took the coat to the old man.

After a while he came back.

"Master, the King didn't like the coat you were married in that the dog sleeps on."

"Oh sour pickle!" cried the innkeeper. "Whatever shall I do?"

"Don't worry," said Little Baggit. "I gave him my coat, and he said that it would do fine."

"Wonderful!" cried the innkeeper. "Little Baggit, you're brighter than a burnt match. Does His Majesty desire anything else?"

"Just your horse, Master. The way to the palace is far and he is tired."

"My horse!" cried the innkeeper. "That old nag isn't fit for a king. Run, Little Baggit, and saddle up the sow."

"The sow? Do you think the King would like that?"

"Of course! Isn't she the finest sow in the country?"

"Well," said Little Baggit, "you know better than I," and he went to saddle the sow.

After a while he came back.

"Master," he said, "the King didn't want to ride the sow."

"Oh sour milk!" cried the innkeeper. "Whatever shall I do?"

"Don't worry," said Little Baggit. "I gave him my donkey, and he said that she would do fine."

"Marvelous!" said the innkeeper. "Your brain would be the envy of a lawyer. I hope the King appreciates all your fine qualities."

"Oh yes," said Little Baggit. "He wants me to come and live with him in the palace."

"My, that is grand," said the innkeeper. "I suppose he'll be coming to fetch you first thing tomorrow in his royal coach."

"I never!" said Little Baggit. "How did you guess? That's just what he said he'd do."

And . . .

That's just what he did.

Brock Cole grew up in the Midwest and attended Kenyon College and the University of Minnesota, where he received his Ph.D. in philosophy. He later taught at the University of Wisconsin. He and his wife, who teaches Greek and Latin at the University of Illinois, now live in Oak Park with their two young sons, where Mr. Cole devotes full-time to painting and to writing and illustrating children's books. *The King at the Door* is his first picture book, and a second one, *No More Baths,* will be published next year.